D1464380

514007-I

Other books by Steve Barlow & Steve Skidmore

Steve Barlow & Steve Skidmore

MIND THE DOOR!

Illustrated by Tony Ross

BARN OWL BOOKS

Mind the Door! was first published by Hamish Hamilton in 1996
This edition is published by Barn Owl Books in 2005
157 Fortis Green Road, London N10 3LX
Barn Owl Books are distributed by Frances Lincoln,
4 Torriano Mews, Torriano Avenue, London NW5 2RZ

ISBN 1-903015-49-9

Designed and typeset by Douglas Martin
Printed and bound in Hong Kong by Imago

Barn Owl Books *gratefully acknowledges*
the financial assistance of Arts Council England
in this publication

Contents

PROLOGUE

The cellar door stood at the bottom of a flight of worn concrete steps, guarded by painted iron railings, behind the school kitchen. For years, nobody had given it a second glance.

When the school was heated by solid fuel, it was different. Then, the cellar door had led to a world of fire and smoke. The two boilers, hunched and massive, sat groaning like chained beasts. The red glow from their fireboxes had made the small cellar into a terrible Underworld, full of the flame and roar of molten lava. You could imagine a Demon King and his imps leaping around bent on mischief, and even hear the shrieks of lost souls, though the caretaker said that was just air in the pipes.

These days the boilers were timid little boxes that ran quietly on gas. The cellar had become the maintenance store; home to buckets, mops, disinfectant, paper towels and rolls of scratchy lavatory paper (special schools issue). The magic of the cellar had gone, and the wooden door with its small panes of frosted glass and peeling green paint was . . . just another door.

But doors are chancy things. When you go though a door, you go from *here* to *there*, and usually the place you end up in is the place you expected to get to.

But not always.

Hidden away in its quiet corner of the school yard, the cellar door waited.

Chapter One

TAKE CARE, CARETAKER

"Parents. Who'd have them?" growled Perce. She kicked a stray ball back into a mêlée of kids trying to kill each other

"Actually, I think they had you. You see, when a mummy loves a daddy very, very much . . ." Andy tailed off as Perce fixed her 'look' on him. "Tell you what, I'll shut up."

"Like this morning," complained Perce, ignoring Andy, "I'm trying to get ready for school when mum starts on me: 'Have you cleaned your room yet?' She knows I haven't. So why ask? What she's really saying is 'Go and tidy your bedroom now!'"

Andy nodded. "My mum says things like that as well. Before tea she *always* asks me: 'Have you washed your hands?' She knows I never have."

"Exactly! What she's really saying is: 'Go and wash them!' So when I pointed out to mum what she was really saying, she said I was being cheeky. Then Dad joined in and that led to a big row and now I've been grounded until I've tidied my room."

"Look on the bright side – it shouldn't take you long."

"You haven't seen my room! I could be there for a million years! Parents!" fumed Perce. "Why can't they be straightforward for once?"

Perce and Andy were standing in a quiet corner of the crowded playground. It was the usual hub-bub of screaming kids. Footballs were being kicked perilously close to windows, "famous player" stickers were being swapped and skipping ropes were cutting the air with whiplash ferocity.

Year one children were being dropped off by protective parents. Scarves were adjusted, brightly coloured plastic lunch boxes handed over and noses wiped.

"You will be good won't you?" one mum whispered as she planted a kiss on a squirming youngster's cheek. Perce glided past, grimaced and hissed. "What she's really saying is: 'You'd better behave or else you're in BIG trouble'." Andy nodded in agreement.

"Another thing about adults is that they never believe anything you say," continued Perce. "Remember when we told them about Ms Dusa?"

Andy considered this. "Latimer believed us."

"Only 'cos he was potty about Greek myths."

Andy grinned "Was. He's not any more!"

This was true, Mr Latimer, the deputy head, had been one of the chief sufferers when Ms Dusa, the supply teacher from hell, had mounted her reign of terror. From being his favourite subject, Greek myths had gone right to the top of Mr Latimer's list of Things-We-Don't-Talk-About.

The school bell pierced through the shrieks and screams of the yard. Crowds of children breathed sighs of relief and surged away from their parents to the sanctuary of the school.

It was then that the man appeared.

Andy saw him first. He gaped. "Look at the size of him!"

Perce whistled softly. "Built like a block of flats."

The man's jacket looked as if someone had taken a doggie-coat off a corgi and put it on a Rottweiler. Every time he moved, it looked about to split along every seam, and when he moved his arms, unseen muscles rippled inside it, like armies of exploring mice.

Perce and Andy stared open mouthed. Other kids also stood still as the man strode towards them. Then they quickly parted. Moses-like, the man moved through them. Dozens of eyes followed him as he continued across the yard, until he disappeared round the side of the school, going towards the kitchen. There was a pause; a collective letting out of breath, then normality returned and kids scooted off to another action-packed, fun-filled day of education.

"Wonder who he is . . . ?" mused Andy. He didn't have time to wonder for too long.

"You TWO!"

A loud yell made Perce and Andy turn. Perce groaned. It was Mr Grimes, the school caretaker – 'Slimey Grimey'. She didn't like him much, but she never let him suspect the fact.

Perce was clever enough to know that school caretakers are the real bosses in any school. Everyone knew which teachers Slimey didn't like. Their classrooms were never dusted, their bins were never emptied and their radiators were turned *off* in winter and *on* in summer. Slimey could make teachers' lives hell. Every Christmas, they would come scurrying to him bearing gifts – usually bottles of whisky – in order to make sure that their year would be trouble free. Sometimes it worked.

"You two, what's that there?"

Andy and Perce followed Slimey's outstretched finger to a piece of paper fluttering about the yard. Andy got on his hands and knees and stared hard at the offending article.

"Eureka!" He straightened and smiled innocently at Slimey. "I believe it is a piece of paper."

Mr Grimes looked as if he would burst. *I know*

its a piece of paper," he snapped. "Pick it up!"

There it was again! Why couldn't adults say what they meant? Perce was too furious to be careful.

"Go break your leg," she muttered.

"I heard that!" Mr Grimes glared. "Right, for that cheek, you can pick up every bit of litter in the yard. Collect it in a bin and then report back to me so I can make sure you've done it."

Andy began to walk away. "Unlucky, Perce," he laughed

"Both of you," yelled Slimey. Andy's smile vanished.

"That was your stupid fault," moaned Perce, as Mr Grimes stomped towards his room. "'Eureka!' Who do you think you are, Aristotle?"

"Me!" exclaimed Andy, "what about you? 'Go break your leg!' Why did you say that?"

Several other stragglers from their class had gathered to snigger at Perce and Andy's plight.

"Actually, Perce, I think you'll find it was Archimedes who said 'Eureka', not Aristotle," said Eddie Johnson.

"Actually, Eddie, I think you'll find my fist up

your nose if you don't shut up!" replied Perce menacingly. Eddie backed away.

"Shall I tell Millsey that you're going to be late?" asked Syreeta.

"Please. Tell her thanks to bozo-brain here," Perce nodded at Andy, "Slimey's got us doing his work for him. She'll understand."

"It wasn't just my fault," muttered Andy defensively.

Well'ard Wally snorted. "It's a good way of getting out of lessons."

"You're never *in* lessons," Perce pointed out.

Well'ard, like Grimes, wasn't the sort to cross or make comments about. He could be considered a trainee caretaker.

"Oh yeah? Well, don't forget to pick these up!" Chuckling, Well'ard helpfully began to empty the contents of his trouser pockets on the playground.

Perce groaned. "Thanks a bunch, Well'ard, you're all heart!"

It took the two of them nearly fifteen minutes to chase the wind-driven litter across the yard, capture it and cage it in the rubbish bin.

They carried the bin (at least, Andy did; Perce supervised) round the corner by the kitchen door, and stood playing "You-go-first-why-me-why-not-you" at the top of the cellar steps. Perce was about to upend the bin over Andy's head when they were both shocked rigid by an almighty crashing noise from behind the cellar door.

Perce's head snapped round. "What was that?"

"Slimey must've kicked the bucket."

Ignoring Andy, Perce pelted down the steps. She couldn't see through the frosted glass panes, but a muffled moaning noise was coming from within.

Andy arrived at her shoulder. "Should we . . .?"

Perce knocked quietly. "Mr Grimes?" She knocked harder. "Mr Grimes, are you there?" She tried the doorknob and pushed against the door.

WHOOSH!

A searing, scorching blast of hot air made Perce and Andy turn their faces and shield their eyes. It seemed to last for an age. When they finally looked in the room, they were confused and dis-orientated.

The usually tidy maintenance store was now a

disorderly, ramshackle mess. Buckets, mops, toilet paper, towels, bottles, canisters and tables were strewn everywhere. Metal shelving was half ripped off the wall and swung erratically. A filing cabinet lay tipped over on its side.

Lying on the floor among the mess was Mr Grimes. He was clutching his leg and moaning. "Horns . . . it was the horns . . . horns . . ."

Andy gave a groan. "Ooer! Look at that!"

He pointed downwards and covered his mouth to stop himself being sick.

Mr Grimes' left leg was bent at an angle that legs were not designed to be bent at.

"Horns, awful horns and fire . . ."

Perce pushed Andy though the door. "Quickly, get help!" she ordered. He scrambled up the steps. Perce turned back to the luckless caretaker. She bit her lip.

"Go break your leg," she had told Mr Grimes. He had.

Chapter Two

THE CARETAKER CARETAKER

" . . . And so I'm sorry to have to tell you," the Head announced in assembly the following day, "that Mr Grimes will not be returning to the school for some time."

The kids listened quietly. Everyone had been shocked by the accident. Slimey hadn't been exactly popular, but he was a familiar figure. Something bad had happened to him in a way that the teachers didn't want to talk about. The pupils sat in uneasy silence, with none of the whispers and bottom-shuffling of a normal assembly.

The Head cleared her throat nervously. She wasn't used to getting the school's undivided attention. "However," she went on, "the news isn't all bad. We've been very fortunate in finding a temporary replacement . . . a sort of caretaker caretaker if you like . . ." The head tittered nervously at her feeble joke; her audience looked blank. "Anyway, I'd like to introduce you to him . . . him to you . . . er, you to each other . . . right away. Would you all say 'good morning' please, to Mr O'Taur."

The Head waved a vague arm to indicate someone at the back. Perce and Andy, along with everyone else, craned their necks round. Whispering broke out.

"Where did he spring from?" Andy hissed in Perce's ear. "He wasn't there when we came in, we'd've noticed. He must've . . . flippin' 'eck!"

The whispers cut off suddenly as Mr O'Taur stood up; "unfolded" was how Perce put it to herself.

There were a few gasps. Perce stared open-mouthed. "It's that bloke," she hissed at Andy. "The one in the yard, yesterday!"

The new caretaker was built on a monstrous scale. Out of his open-necked sports shirt sprouted a tree-trunk of a neck. His head was in proportion with the rest of him. He had a solid jaw and a wide mouth; his eyes were small and hidden in the fold between high cheekbones and a low forehead, on which sat eyebrows like giant hairy caterpillars. His hair was a mass of jet-black curls. But the most unusual feature was his nose. It was large and flattish, and wouldn't have been particularly noticeable except for the fact that he had a nose ring in it.

Funny, thought Perce. Caretakers aren't supposed to be trendy!

A voice from deep inside Mr O'Taur rumbled, "Good morning."

The school's answering "Good morning" was a shambles. The awkward silence that followed was only ended by the Head's hurried dismissal.

Perce's mind was racing. For some reason that had nothing to do with his size, she didn't like the look of the new caretaker. What had he been doing at the school yesterday before . . . she gave the big man a hard stare . . . before Slimey had his accident?

Mr O'Taur left as the first years filed out. Perce turned to Andy and raised her eyebrows. Andy licked his lips and tried to look unconcerned.

"Looks a bit of a bully to me," he said.

"Witch!"

Well'ard Wally's voice grated in Perce's ear. She swung round to glare at him.

"Who is?"

"You are." Miss Mills was busy in the stock cupboard, so Well'ard had stopped even pretending to work. He raised his voice. "Oi! You lot! Perce is a witch!"

"How d'you reckon that?" demanded Andy.

Well'ard grinned. "When Slimey made you pick up that paper, Perce said 'Go break your leg', and he did, so that proves it."

Eddie Johnson looked dubious. "No it doesn't. Witches have pointy hats and black cats and broomsticks and they dance round in convents."

"Covens," said Andy. "Convents is nuns."

"Well, they dance anyway."

"I heard they dance round wi' no clothes on," leered Well'ard. "D'you dance around in the nuddy, Perce?"

Perce gave Well'ard one of her best laser-mega-death looks. He just grinned at her. Well'ard hadn't got to be the school hard case by worrying about looks from Perce.

"Hey, what if Perce is a witch?" Eddie's imagination was getting into top gear. "We could have her in a tent at the school fair . . ."

"Madame Priscilla, Fortune-teller," agreed Syreeta. Perce winced. She hated it when people used her full name.

Others joined in. "With a tea-towel round her bonce."

"Reading palms."

"And tea-leaves."

"What're tea-leaves?" asked somebody whose tea came in bags.

"And looking into her crystal ball."

"Is there anybody therrrrre?" moaned Well'ard with his eyes shut.

"Yes, there is." Miss Mills appeared in the doorway having finally tracked down the school's only working staple gun. "What's all this noise about?"

"It's Andy, Miss." Well'ard ignored Andy's protests. "He says Perce is a witch."

Miss Mills snorted. "Superstitious nonsense. There are no such things as witches. They're just a myth." Perce jumped as if she'd been shot. "Now get on with your work."

For the rest of the morning, every time Miss Mills's attention was elsewhere, Well'ard would start chanting, "Witch . . . witch . . . witch," just loud enough for Perce to hear, but he needn't have bothered. Perce wasn't listening. A small but persistent thought was tugging at the coat-sleeve of her mind and she didn't get much work done for the rest of the day.

"Where are we going?" Andy had to trot to keep up with Perce as she charged down the corridor after school.

"To see Mr Latimer."

"What?" Andy stopped dead and goggled at her. "Well, if that's your idea of a fun time . . ."

"You needn't come." Perce hadn't even slowed down.

Sighing, Andy followed.

They found Mr Latimer trying to get a computer trolley up the step into his classroom. He didn't look too pleased to see them.

"Could we see you, sir?"

"You *are* seeing me."

This wasn't exactly encouraging, but Perce pressed on. "We wanted to ask you something."

"What's all this 'we'?" muttered Andy, and got a sharp nudge from Perce's elbow.

"Well, what is it?" Mr Latimer lifted the trolley over the step. A wheel fell off.

"It's about myths, sir. You know, Greek myths."

Mr Latimer glowered. "That is not a subject I wish to be reminded of, Priscilla."

"But, sir . . ."

"School is over. This is my free time, and I'd rather not spend it discussing unpleasant topics, so if you don't mind . . ."

"But, sir . . ."

". . . or even if you do." Mr Latimer dragged the trolley into his room with a clatter, and closed the door in a very marked manner. Perce seethed.

"Silly old fool, I hope he breaks his . . ."

"Don't say it!" Andy looked alarmed.

Perce glared at him in disgust. "Not you, too."

Andy gave a sheepish grin.

"Come on."

Again, Andy had to trot to keep up. "Where are we going now?"

"The hospital."

"Hospital? I don't want to go to the hospital?"

Perce clenched her fist. "You have a choice. You can go as a visitor or as a patient . . ."

"I know, lets go to the hospital."

"Hello, Mr Grimes."

The face on the pillow didn't look much like Slimey's; it was older and thinner than Perce remembered. For a moment, Mr Grimes looked at them without recognition. Then he said, "Oh . . . it's Perce, isn't it? And Arthur . . ."

"Andy. We brought you these." Andy held out a bunch of flowers, quietly harvested from the local park on their way to the hospital. Then he started feeling stupid, because there wasn't a vase or anything to put them in

Mr Grimes forced a smile. "Ta." He waved a

hand vaguely. "Just leave them on the table here, one of the nurses will see to them later."

Andy laid down their limp offering, and Perce sat on the hard chair by the bed, glancing round nervously. She hated hospitals.

"Er . . . how are you?"

"Oh, mustn't grumble." Mr Grimes' left leg, smothered in plaster, was held up off the bed by a complicated system of slings.

"Does it hurt?" asked Andy. Perce glared at him.

"Only when I'm awake."

There was an awkward silence.

"Well, it's nice of you to visit me," said Mr Grimes. "I haven't had many visitors . . ."

"Mr Grimes," blurted Perce, leaning forward anxiously, when we found you, after the accident, you were muttering something . . ."

The pain in Mr Grimes' eyes mingled with a look of astonishment "Was I?"

Perce took the plunge. "You were saying something about . . . horns."

Mr Grimes frowned. "Horns? I . . ." His eyes widened and he stared at Perce.

"Yes, I remember . . . it must have been the

shock, I suppose. Hallucinations. Just for a moment, down there in the cellar, I could've sworn I saw this huge figure, like a man . . . but . . ."

Perce bit her lip. "Yes?"

"But with a bull's horns."

A twinge of pain made Mr Grimes close his eyes. When he opened them again, the chair by the bed was empty. The ward doors swung widely to and fro.

Perce and Andy had gone.

Chapter Three

MYTH ILLOGICAL

"So what are you trying to say to me?"

Perce hadn't said a word on the way back from the hospital. In the schoolyard next morning, she was in a foul humour and Andy couldn't get any sense out of her.

"I'm saying there's something dead weird going on," said Perce darkly. "Slimey said he saw a monster with a bull's horns."

"Oh, come on!" scoffed Andy. "He nips in the cellar, and this mad bull leaps on him and breaks his leg. I don't think so."

Perce wasn't used to this sort of opposition from Andy. "Listen, jelly-brain, why would he say he saw horns if he didn't?"

"It was probably a shadow."

"A *what?*"

Andy and Perce joined the pushing, shoving line of their classmates heading for the door.

"You know, like you get in horror films, where someone's all alone in some dark creepy place and the music goes dah-dah-dah-DAH! and they turn round and there's a huge shadow on the wall of this 'orrible sabre-tooth wotsit about to tear their throat out and they go 'Aaaaargh!': only then it comes out of the light and it's really a fluffy kitten."

Several people were now staring at Andy. He shrugged. "Or he might've been delirious."

Perce snorted. "You've got a nerve calling anyone else delirious after all that rubbish about fluffy sabre-tooth kittens."

"Well, I reckon if I'd just had my leg broken in

umpteen places, I'd be deliri . . . Wow!"

Perce and Andy gawped open-mouthed. All down the corridor, kids were staring in disbelief.

The school *gleamed*.

The grimy plaster and dull woodwork were suddenly bright and fresh. Windows sparkled, the wood-block floor shone, there wasn't a sweet wrapper, a lump of fluff or even a speck of dust *anywhere*.

It was the same in their classroom. Miss Mills was wandering round in a daze trying to find things, but it wasn't as if anything was lost or out of place. She just didn't recognise the shining globe, the spotless water pots or the neat felt-tips as the battered, sticky, dusty objects she had put away the night before. Even the computer keyboard, blackened from constant use by thousands of grubby fingers, gleamed as if fresh out of the box. You could even read the letters now. Which, as Perce later pointed out, took half the fun out of it.

Andy still looked like a startled goldfish. "Look at this lot! It must have taken him all night!"

Perce stared at him. "*All night*? He couldn't have done it if he'd worked all *week*, not if he was

Superman. Some of that dirt was older than me. Some of it was older than *Latimer!*"

There was one new addition to the room. Slap in the middle of the notice board was a poster on yellow paper with bold black lettering:

Coming soon!
SCHOOL ATHLETICS CLUB
IN THE SCHOOL HALL
TUESDAYS AND THURSDAYS 4-6 PM
Get fit, not fat
LEADER: MR E. O'TAUR

Perce studied the poster for some time, considering. She muttered "O'Taur" under her breath a few times. Then she turned to Andy. "We're going to the library first lesson, right?"

Andy glanced at the class timetable on the wall. "Right."

"Good. There's something I want to check."

In the library, Perce made a bee-line for one of the shelves. Without a moment's hesitation, she picked out a book. Andy, curious, read the title: *Myths of Ancient Greece*.

Perce riffled through the book until she found the page she was looking for. She read a section with great concentration, occasionally nodding to herself. Andy was baffled.

Eventually, Perce turned to Andy with a fixed, determined look and held the book open under his nose. Andy shrugged, spread the book out flat, and started to read:

The Legend of the Minotaur

Minos, a strong and cruel king, ruled the island of Crete. He forced King Aegeus of Athens to send him a tribute of seven young men and seven young women of Athens. Their fate was to be sacrificed to a dreadful monster, which lived in the great Labyrinth below Minos's palace at Knossos. This monster had the body of a man, but the head of a bull. It was called the Minotaur . . .

Andy turned towards Perce. She was staring at the picture on the opposite page. It showed the Minotaur, a huge and horrifying creature with knotted muscles, a thick neck and a mane of jet-black hair.

"So? Why are you showing me this?"

Perce stared at him. Then she started to explain very slowly and carefully, as though speaking to a very small child: "Because it's about the Minotaur." She paused. "Mine-otaur." She waited for Andy to catch on. He looked blank. "Mr. Mine. O'Taur."

Andy's eyes bulged as the penny dropped. Then, to Perce's amazement, he started to giggle.

"Oh, leave it out, Perce. You're bein' illogical." Andy paused momentarily, before breaking into a huge grin. "In fact, you're being mythillogical — myth illogical. Geddit?"

From this point on, the conversation became rather strained.

Andy pointed out that Perce wouldn't expect to see Hercules nipping down the Taj Mahal take-away for a chicken vindaloo, would she? She wouldn't find the Wooden Horse of Troy holding up traffic outside Tesco's. Even a thicko like Perce ought to see that things like that didn't happen.

Perce retorted that O'Taur had appeared on the

same day that Slimey had had his accident. Perhaps Andy could explain *that* if he was so clever. And while he was about it, could Andy (World's Number One Genius – NOT!) explain the blast of heat when he and Perce had opened the cellar door?

The World's Number One Genius replied that all the evidence indicated that Perce was stark raving mad; in reply to which Perce invited the World's Number One Genius to step outside and say that again, and offered to telephone for an ambulance and a couple of bottles of blood.

The World's Number One Genius told her to get knotted.

"Anyway," boiled Perce, "what about his name?"

Andy sneered. "Coincidence. I bet there's lots of O'Taurs. It's probably the second most common Irish name after O'Toole or something."

Perce seethed. "And he's got a nose ring! That's what bulls have."

"So do people," Andy snapped back. "Anyway, that's nothing. My uncle Simon's got a safety pin through his nose . . . and through both ears."

Perce grabbed Andy by the shoulder and shoved

his face towards the book. "Look at the picture. Doesn't it remind you of anyone?"

Andy squinted. "Not really. The bloke in this picture's got horns for a start."

"Yeah, well . . ." Perce bit her lip. She hadn't worked that point out herself yet.

"He couldn't hide them. I mean, either he's got horns or he hasn't . . ."

"All right, Einstein. We'll see. We're going to keep an eye on Mr O'Taur and find out what he's up to . . ."

"Who's this 'we'?"

". . . and we can start at the gym club tonight."

Chapter Four

MYSTERY O'TAUR

"I'm not going! I don't see why I should go just because you want to go!"

Perce and Andy were still arguing as they stood in the dinner queue.

"I don't *want* to go," Perce pointed out acidly. "But we've *got* to go to keep an eye on him."

"There you go with the 'we' stuff again," Andy complained, "I don't want to keep an eye on him.

I'm not the nutso who thinks the bloke who empties the waste-paper bins is a bull in a boiler suit.
Sausage roll and chips please," he added as he
reached the service hatch.

"You don't want chips." Perce shoved Andy to
one side. "He doesn't want chips."

"Yes, I do!" protested Andy.

"No you don't. You've got to lose weight for the
gym club."

Perce selected a salad for herself and steered a
mutinous Andy to an empty table, where, much
to her disgust, Well'ard and Eddie Johnson joined
them a few seconds later.

"You two joinin' the gym club, then?" asked
Eddie through a mouthful of chips.

"No!" said Andy, eyeing Eddie's chips ravenously.

"Yes!" Perce kicked him under the table. "Both
of us."

"What? Andy's doin' gym club?" Well'ard did a
bad imitation of a faint and knocked over Perce's
orange juice. "Andy gets hot flushes taking the top
off his biro. Every time he sharpens his pencil, he
needs a lie-down after."

Andy went into a sulk.

"Well'ard's comin' too," said Eddie.

Perce stopped mopping juice. "Get out of town!"

Well'ard did a muscle-man pose. "Thought I'd show you how it's done."

"You must be joking." Perce stared at Well'ard. "You've never done PE in your life, you always bring a note."

"Yeah, well, that's a matter of principle gettin' out of PE," explained Well'ard. "But keep fit's different. You've gotta be fit to get in the SAS."

Perce groaned. Well'ard had told everyone in the class at least fifty times that he was going to join the SAS.

Well'ard continued to explain his momentous decision. "Anyway, that new bloke looks like he knows how to get people fit. Couple of weeks with him, even Andy might be able to bend a stick of liquorice." Well'ard pushed his plate away and wandered off, nudging people to make them spill their food as he went.

"What's SAS stand for anyway?" asked Eddie, finishing his last chip.

"Stupid And Sad," muttered Perce, glaring after Well'ard.

Even before the Gym Club started, it was clear that, as far as the staff were concerned, Mr O'Taur could do no wrong. Teachers who in Perce's view, ought to have been kept in cages, purred like pussy cats whenever the caretaker was around. There was hardly any litter. A discarded crisp packet stood out like a giraffe on an iceberg.

Everything was so clean and ran so well that few people noticed – or cared – that the new caretaker was very rarely about. Slimey had always been pottering around the school, but Mr O'Taur only seemed to put in an appearance when there was a particular job to be done. Occasionally he was glimpsed going down the steps to his store in the old cellar, but apart from that nobody seemed to be bothered about where he spent most of his time. Nobody, that is, except Perce.

"I want to know what he does in there!" she said.

"If he wants to sit in the cellar all day," Andy snapped in exasperation, "that's up to him. Maybe he's making a papier mâché model of the Royal Family out of toilet rolls."

"Don't be stupid," said Perce. "He's up to something."

"Why should he be up to anything?"

"Because he's the Minotaur!"

"You keep saying that," complained Andy, "but he's not doing anything except keep the school clean. What makes you so sure?"

"Well, there's his name, for a start . . ."

"Oh, his *name*," sneered Andy. "Yes, his last name, we've heard about that, what about his first name?"

Perce scowled. This was another weak spot in her argument, and she knew it.

"His first name starts with an 'E'." Andy pressed home his advantage. "It's on all the gym club posters. What d'you reckon it stands for? The Eric O'Taur? The Eddie O'Taur? The Ernest O'Taur. Or maybe, the Egbert-no-bacon O'Taur?" Perce chewed her lip and said nothing. "Come on, Perce, let's forget the gym club . . ."

"We are going," said Perce, twisting Andy's arm, "to the gym club."

"Get off, that hurts." Andy rubbed his arm and said bitterly, "You haven't got any arguments. You're just in a bad mood because you think I might be right."

To that, Perce said nothing. Mostly because it was true.

The gym club was a lot better than Perce and Andy had expected. There was a good turnout. Eddie was there in fluorescent-pink cycling shorts and so was Well'ard dressed in his dad's old rugby shorts and last year's trainers. About thirty other kids turned up.

Mr O'Taur was professionally kitted out in an expensive-looking tracksuit. He was very business-like; he just explained what he wanted the group to do, clapped his hands once, and let them get on. He never wasted words, and he never raised his voice. He never needed to.

One reason for this was that nobody felt like cheeking someone who looked quite capable of tearing pianos apart with his bare hands, and another was that the exercises were fun. There were sit-ups and stretching exercises and push-ups, all the usual things; nevertheless Mr O'Taur managed to turn everything into a game – a game where everyone felt they'd won. He changed the activity before anyone got bored or tired out and he never forced anyone to do anything. He never praised anyone, but he never criticized either. Perce and Andy finished the first session feeling fresher than when they'd started.

"It's not right," Perce muttered darkly, "I should feel knackered, but I don't."

Andy sniffed. "You're just looking for something to moan about. That was brill!"

In the following sessions, the exercises became more complicated and tougher, but even unsporty types like Eddie started to feel fitter and more confident, and proud of their new skills.

Perce began to feel less sure of herself. Maybe she had made a mistake about Mr O'Taur. It still seemed wrong to Perce that she suddenly found herself doing the sort of gymnastics she'd never have dreamt of being able to do – the sort you should only be able to do if you weighed three stones and came from China. But she was doing them, and so were Andy, Well'ard, Eddie and all the others, and it felt good, so what was she worrying about? Maybe Andy was right after all.

Then, three things happened.

The first was a delivery. A van pulled up at the front entrance during morning break. Curious kids watched as two sweating delivery-men and Mr O'Taur manoeuvred a large, heavy object wrapped in layers of bubble film into the school. By lunch-time, the school's new acquisition had been unpacked, and Perce and Andy watched as Mr O'Taur strolled round it, lovingly stroking the leather hide. It stood in the middle of the hall, its four splayed wooden legs giving it a slightly comic air that was also, at least to Perce, a little disturbing. It was a huge vaulting-horse.

The second thing happened a few minutes later; Mr O'Taur spotted Perce hanging around and gave her the delivery-note that had come with the horse to take to the school secretary. Halfway down the corridor, Perce stopped so suddenly that Andy, who had been following, bumped into her. She was staring at the note. Without a word, she shoved it under Andy's nose.

Andy examined the note, and then looked enquiringly at Perce.

"Look at the signature!"

Mr O'Taur had signed to say that he had received the delivery. There was his name in his neat, surprisingly small handwriting. 'Emmanuel O'Taur'.

Andy still didn't get it.

"Emmanuel," Perce explained slowly, her voice shaking with suppressed excitement. "Not Eric, or Eddie, or Ernest: Emmanuel. If you're called Emmanuel, d'you know what people call you for short?"

Andy shook his head. He didn't know anyone called Emmanuel.

"They call you Manny," said Perce, rolling the word round her tongue. "Manny. Manny O'Taur.

"The third thing happened a couple of days later. Nobody saw it happen, and for some time, nobody even knew that it had.

It started with an argument. Lee Adams said that gym club had been cancelled because of a parents' evening. Syreeta said the Head had decided that the gym club could go ahead as usual.

They were still arguing as the bell went, so Lee said they should go and ask Mr O'Taur. He would probably be in the store, and if they hurried they wouldn't be too late for registration.

Nobody saw them go down the cellar steps and hesitate in front of the green door.

"Mr O'Taur?" called Syreeta.

The cellar door swung open. A rumbling sound came from inside. It might have been a very deep voice saying, "Come in."

Syreeta hung back but Lee gave her a scornful look and stepped through the doorway, so then of course Syreeta had to go in too.

The cellar door swung closed behind them.

Chapter Five

IT'S YOUR VAULT

There *was* a gym club that night – a special one. When the kids walked into the gym, there in the middle was the new vaulting-horse. Mr O'Taur stood next to it patting and stroking the leather top.

"It looks just like an animal," whispered Perce to Andy. "All that leather, just like a . . ."

"Don't tell me . . ." Andy shook his head. "Let

me guess. You're going to say 'like a bull'. You're right, it does — apart from the horns . . . and the tail . . . and the face . . . and the . . . ow!" Perce stared hard at Andy. Andy rubbed his shoulder. "I wish you'd stop doing that," he grimaced.

"Don't be sarcastic then."

"Sit down!" Their squabbling was interrupted by Mr O'Taur's deep voice.

The kids immediately settled down and listened attentively as Mr O'Taur began to explain how to vault. "Run fast at the horse, bounce on the springboard, keep your legs wide apart, place your hands in the middle of the horse and vault over it to land on the other side." The instructions were delivered in a matter-of-fact voice and a this-is-so-simple-you-can-all-do-it manner. "When you have mastered this, we will progress to more complicated and *interesting* leaps and vaults."

"What's he mean by interesting?" hissed Perce. As if in answer to her seemingly unheard question, Mr O'Taur suddenly sprinted at the horse, launched himself at the front end and soared upwards. As he floated in mid air, he twisted and flipped his body round once . . . twice . . . three times. This sent him spinning over the horse in a perfect arc. His spiralling descent and two footed landing were achieved with a grace and an ease that seemed unnatural.

There was silence. The kids stared, aghast. Even Perce was impressed: Mr O'Taur hadn't even bothered to use the springboard.

"I don't expect you to do that straight away," Mr O'Taur smiled. The kids chuckled at the joke. "It is an example of what you can do with practice. Years and years of it," he added. "Now, get into line."

The next hour was filled with hurtling bodies and loud cheers and applause as kids leaped, sprang and vaulted over the horse as best they could. The whole gym was buzzing with a concentrated excitement. Despite herself, Perce was lost in the thrill of defeating gravity for a split second.

Even Eddie Johnson's unfortunate mishap couldn't dampen the enthusiasm for vaulting. It happened on his third vault: he ran hard at the springboard, leapt two footed on it and bounced over the front of the horse, legs splayed.

Unfortunately he forgot to put his hands down, in order to leapfrog the horse, and he landed, legs wide apart, in the middle of the hard leather top.

THUMP!

Eddie's lips pursed and both his pupils shot towards his nose. A pleading, squeaking sound came from somewhere deep inside as he fought for breath.

It was one of those incidents that would normally have had everyone laughing like hyenas but no one did: except for Well'ard who laughed at everything.

"I bet he can sing soprano now!" he chortled. "I reckon he's gonna be well bruised on his –"

"Silence!" ordered Mr O'Taur. Well'ard shut up. Mr O'Taur turned to Eddie. "Hard luck, lad, try again."

A week or two ago, Eddie would have howled and gone home. Today, he staggered cross-eyed and cross-legged to the back of the line ready for another attempt.

The vaulting continued.

Towards the end of the session as they stood waiting their turn, Andy turned to Perce. "Shame that Syreeta and Lee missed this today. They'd have enjoyed it."

"Yeah," nodded Perce.

"Wonder what's wrong with them?"

"They're skivin'," said Well'ard, who'd been ear-wigging the conversation.

"How do you know that?" asked Perce.

"I saw them this morning," said Well'ard. "I told Millsey I'd seen them and I reckoned that they were skivin', but she didn't believe me."

"I wonder why?" Perce's sarcasm was hardly subtle.

Well'ard returned her stare. "You sayin' I tell lies?"

"Well'ard," replied Perce, "if they gave medals for lying you'd win the Olympic gold."

Well'ard huffed a snort of hurt disapproval and put on his world-famous wounded puppy look. Perce felt a twang of conscience. Maybe Well'ard *was* telling the truth. Also, she was curious to know about Lee and Syreeta. Against her better judgement she decided to give Well'ard the benefit of the doubt.

"All right Well'ard, where did you see them? If

you saw them at all," she added to let him know she was still not convinced.

Well'ard turned from his position at the front of the line of vaulters. He gave Perce a told-you-so look before replying. "They were in the yard near Mr O'Taur's office." He turned to face the vaulting horse: "GERANIUM!"

"Geronimo," corrected Eddie in a strangled voice. His eyes were still watering.

"Yeah, him an' all," replied Well'ard as he sprinted for the horse, arms and legs flailing the air.

"Nice style," commented Andy, "Dead elegant."

"More like a dead elephant," wheezed Eddie.

Perce ignored them. "Near Mr O'Taur's office?"

"Come on. Perce!" Andy nudged her. "It's your turn."

Perce looked over to the horse where Mr O'Taur stood waiting. He was beckoning towards her.

"Oh . . . er . . . you go next, Andy. I think I've just pulled a muscle."

"By standing still?" Andy shrugged his shoulders and began sprinting towards the waiting horse.

Perce didn't have to vault again. After Andy had completed his vault, Mr O'Taur clapped his hands.

"That's it. Stretching-out exercises."

As the kids began stretching their legs and arms Mr O'Taur walked among them checking that they were warming down properly.

"Good," he said. "Now, listen carefully." He touched several of the kids on the head. "Robert Williams, Justin Green, Nitesh Patel, Sam Skinner, Oliver Moore and Delroy Peters. You have all worked very well tonight and show a lot of potential." The named kids began to glow with pride. "As a reward you can stay behind and help me put away the vaulting-horse." There were groans, but not from the six "volunteers" they were honoured at being chosen. It was the rest of the group who were disappointed. Everyone except Perce. Normally she would have moaned about how sexist it was that only boys had been asked to put something heavy away, but tonight she wanted to get out of the gym as quickly as possible.

"The rest of you," thundered Mr O'Taur, "Off you go."

Perce was the first out of the door.

Chapter Six

ABSENT FRIENDS

The alarm bells in Perce's head were ringing full blast next day. Lee and Syreeta were still away. Perce had waited anxiously for them in the schoolyard before registration, but they hadn't appeared. Miss Mills asked if anyone knew anything about their absence when she took the register.

"They're skivin' again!" Well'ard shouted out, but Miss Mills waved him away with a dismissive:

"Yes thank you, Walter." Well'ard sat back in his chair and folded his arms grumpily.

"Now, sit still everyone while I get some paper."

As Miss Mills headed to the stock cupboard, Perce turned to Andy. "They're away again."

"So?"

"So, it's obvious isn't it?"

"Yeah, it's obvious that they're ill," Andy said sarcastically."For instance, they may have broken their legs, got a cold . . ."

"But, Andy . . ."

". . . caught mumps . . ."

"Andy . . ."

". . . got bumps . . ."

"Andy . . ."

" . . .suffered lumps." Andy was now in full rapping mode.

"ANDY!" screamed Perce. "What if O'Taur has done something to Lee and Syreeta!"

"Priscilla! Why are you shouting?" Miss Mills stormed back into the room. Perce didn't have time to respond. "And why haven't you started to collect the registers? It's your turn, hurry up."

Perce stared at Andy; he smirked back. Going

round all the classrooms to collect the registers and the lists of people who were absent was supposed to be a treat, but Perce found it a chore. She headed off towards Mr Latimer's classroom with Miss Mills' register and absence list. On it were Lee and Syreeta's names. Perce shook her head and began worrying again.

Twenty minutes later, Perce stood outside the school secretary's office. Not bad she thought, if you've got to do a boring job, then waste as much time as possible doing it.

"Won't be a minute," called Mrs Robbins, the secretary.

"Take as long as you want," mumbled Perce. As she stood waiting, she flicked through the absence lists.

Lee and Syreeta from Perce's class.

Robert Williams from Mr Latimer's class.

Justin Green from Ms Paine's.

None from Mrs "What-a-Dragon" Needit's class. No one would dare be away, thought Perce. Mr White's class – Nitesh Patel and Sam Skinner. Perce stopped flicking – where had she recently heard those names?

Oliver Moore from Mrs Jones's . . .

Perce went very cold. She glanced quickly through the other lists . . . and found what she was half expecting and half hoping she wouldn't. Absent from Miss Smith's class – Delroy Peters.

"Everyone Mr O'Taur chose to help put away the vaulting horse last night is away today!" Perce yelled at Andy at break-time.

"Perce . . ." sighed Andy.

"All six of them are on the absent list."

"Coincidence?" suggested Andy.

"Coincidence!" Perce shouted back at him. "He's *done* something to them; like he's done something to Lee and Syreeta!"

"Oh come off it, Perce, where's your proof?" Andy was fed up with Perce going on about Mr O'Taur.

"The volunteers are away after he asked them to stay behind; Lee and Syreeta were seen near his store-room; his name and . . . and . . ." Perce was running out of steam, "he's really different and strange!"

"If being strange makes you a mythological

monster," Andy snapped back, "then all teachers, my parents, and most adults are mythological monsters – and so are you!"

"Andy . . ."

"You're being stupid. Mythological monsters don't go round being nice and cleaning schools and running gym clubs! And another thing – if they were missing, their parents would have gone to the police."

"Maybe O'Taur uses hypnosis to make them think things are normal, like Dusa did."

"Oh, come off it."

Although he was tired of hearing Perce's unfounded accusations, there was another reason why Perce's suspicions about Mr O'Taur annoyed Andy. It was one which he would never have thought possible: he was enjoying the gym sessions! The new vaulting-horse was brilliant! And the way that Mr O'Taur coached, persuaded and encouraged everyone was great. Mr O'Taur was rapidly becoming Andy's hero.

"Perce, you're just being paranormal!" Andy waved his arms and shook his head "Watch out! Watch out! The walls are closing in, everybody!"

Perce gave him a look of contempt. "You mean, paranoid."

Andy hated it when Perce corrected him. "Okay, paranoid," he snarled. "Why don't you go and take a running jump off a parapet?" The air between the two of them was now more than frosty, it was positively Arctic.

"Ha ha," sneered Perce. "Talking of 'para' words, you're going to need a *para*medic in a minute!"

"Oh yeah!" Andy stared straight into Perce's eyes. "I'm fed up with you threatening me all the time. Just 'cos you're a girl you think you can pick on me!" The ferocity of his voice shocked Perce into being unable to think of a reply.

"I'm sick of you," Andy continued, "You always think you're right. Always telling me what to do, always telling me what to think. Just because Syreeta and Lee are skiving off school, you have to blame O'Taur, 'cos it fits in with your stupid ideas! Well I think O'Taur's all right! He's not a monster, he's brilliant! I like *him* and I don't like *you*!"

Perce was stunned by Andy's attack. She felt her face beginning to flush and tears welling up in her eyes.

"I'm not walking home with you anymore. So forget tomorrow morning: I'll walk to school on my own!" Andy stormed away and headed for the football game taking place in the yard.

Perce stood flabbergasted. Tears began to trickle down her face. She'd never argued like this with Andy before. She fought back further tears and gritted her teeth. She wasn't someone to admit that she was wrong. "All right, I'll prove it to you!" she shouted. She wiped her tears away as some passing year ones began to point at her and laugh. Perce realized that she was making a spectacle of herself and needed to regain her composure. She covered her face and ran off, head down, towards the toilets.

If Perce had looked up, as she dashed across the playground, she would have seen Mr O'Taur standing in the corner of the yard by the kitchens, surveying the scene. As she ran into the toilets, Mr O'Taur smiled, turned, made his way down the cellar steps and disappeared into his store-room.

At lunch-time, Perce made another visit to the school library. It was empty apart from the librarian, and Well'ard and Eddie, who were sitting at one of the computers.

Perce searched the shelves for several minutes. Then she approached the desk and said, "Excuse me, Mrs Jones," in her 'please-help-me-as-I'm-totally-useless' voice.

"Yes?" snapped Mrs Jones, clearly thinking that her library would be a nice, quiet, orderly place if only kids wouldn't keep coming in to borrow books.

"I'm looking for the book on Greek myths. I can't find it on the shelf."

"Then it must be out!"

"When is it due back?" enquired Perce sweetly.

"Just a minute." Glowering, Mrs Jones checked the card files. "It's out on a long term loan," she eventually announced.

"Oh!" Perce was disappointed. "I needed it for a project. Who's got it out?"

Mrs Jones peered at the ticket. Even before she replied, Perce knew what the answer was going to be.

"Mr O'Taur."

Perce's stomach lurched. She mumbled a

"thanks" and turned away. Then a thought struck her. She hurried over to the set of encyclopedias and picked out the *Man to Myth* volume.

Sitting at a table, she began to flick through the pages looking for 'Minotaur'. After a few seconds she stopped and stared in horror. She flipped several pages back and forward, but there was no mistake.

The page in the encyclopedia that must have contained the entry on the Minotaur had been ripped out!

By now thoroughly alarmed, Perce went over to Well'ard and Eddie, who were surfing the net. It was probably best not to enquire what they were up to – Well'ard had once tried to sell the school on e-bay. Perce wasn't interested anyway. "Search for 'Minotaur'," she told Eddie.

Something about the look on her face made Eddie hurry to obey. Even Well'ard didn't ask questions. The search results came up. Eddie selected a site.

An error message appeared. *The page cannot be displayed.*

Eddie shrugged, and selected another site. The

same message appeared.

Well'ard sniggered. "That's what it does when you try to look at naughty photos."

Perce glared at him. "How do you know?"

"I heard," said Well'ard hastily.

"He's right," said Eddie. He continued to select sites. All were unavailable. "There's a firewall on these computers to stop us looking at things we're not supposed to see. Somebody must have fiddled with it to stop us looking up stuff on the Minotaur." He gave Perce a puzzled look. "Why would anybody do that?"

Perce stared at the screen. "I don't know. But I can guess."

Chapter Seven

A BULL BY THE HORNS

"What's wrong with you?" asked Perce's father.

Ha! thought Perce. What you mean is, "Stop sulking or I'll give you something to sulk about."

"Is something the matter, love?"

Perce looked up. Her mum must have been reading that book on 'Good Parenting' again.

"School," she said. That usually cut off further enquiries; parents never wanted to know what happened at school, it was bad enough coping with what happened at home.

"Homework, is it?" Perce nodded. That was safe. She knew she couldn't tell her mum about Mr O'Taur. "I've got to do a project on a Greek myth, but all the books are out and I couldn't get on line at school and our computer's not working."

Her father grunted. "Well who spilled cola all over the keyboard?"

"All right dad, don't go on. This is important."

"Why not try the town library?"

Perce inwardly kicked herself. She's been so upset she hadn't thought of that. Of course! Mr O'Taur could hardly have ripped out every reference to the Minotaur in the main library – or got at their Internet browser. She checked the clock.

"I can't go now, it'll be shut."

"What do you have to find out?"

Perce stared. Her dad hadn't offered to help her with homework since she'd presented him with a maths problem that had made him chew his tie and swear in frustration. He'd spent hours wrestling with it. He'd nearly throttled Perce when she moaned at him next day for getting the answer wrong.

"Well . . ." Perce hesitated, ". . . it's about the Minotaur."

"That's the one with Theseus, isn't it?"

Perce gaped. Her dad actually knew something!

"Er, yes . . . well, all I know so far is that the Minotaur lived in a labyrinth. What's a labyrinth?"

"Well, it's a sort of . . . it's like a . . . you get them . . ." her father was clearly already regretting his helpful impulse. Explaining things to Perce always gave him a headache. "It's a sort of maze."

"Like that famous one at Hampton Court near London – the one made out of hedges . . .?"

"No. More like tunnels. Underground."

Light dawned. Perce stared at him as the picture of a certain green wooden door with frosted panes of glass sprang into her mind. "You mean, like a cellar?"

Next day, Perce did some checking around. None of her missing schoolmates had returned. Andy was still ignoring her. How could she find out what O'Taur was up to?

The answer came to her at break when Well'ard asked Perce whether she was going to the gym club that afternoon.

Perce's eyes gleamed. Of course! While the gym club was on, she knew where O'Taur would be. She had to discover what was going on in the cellar, and this was her chance!

After lessons had ended, she went out into the playground, tiptoed up to the gym wall, and peered through the window. Inside, there was a line of children taking it in turns to vault. Andy, Well'ard and Eddie were all there. As usual there was no fuss, no noise, just a studied concentration.

There was a change to the vaulting-horse. It horrified Perce, though she couldn't have said why. Since the last session, Mr O'Taur had fitted what looked like a pair of motorbike handlebars to the front of the horse, so that it looked as if it had grown . . . Perce gulped . . . horns.

Mr O'Taur issued his commands. Each pupil took it in turns to run at the horse, jump on the springboard and vault; but now, the more adventurous ones were doing handflicks from the handlebar-horns. After each jump, Mr O'Taur would offer criticism tempered with expert advice. Once or twice he even demonstrated a vault himself, using the horns as handgrips and somersaulting over the horse with ease.

Perce turned away. She hadn't been seen and her presence seemed not to have been missed at the club. She began to head across the playground towards the cellar door.

A burst of applause came from the gym. Perce glanced back over her shoulder. Someone must have done a good leap, she thought. At least she knew where O'Taur was.

She crept down the steps to the green wooden door and stood before it, her hand poised over the doorknob. She peered through the frosted panes but could see nothing. This is it, she thought, here goes. Her hand moved downwards and took a firm grip on the brass doorknob.

Perce half expected the door to be locked. If she was being truthful with herself, she was half hoping it *would* be. It wasn't. The doorknob turned. She pushed against the door and it began to glide open. Shaking, she pushed the door fully open and stepped inside.

What Perce expected to see and what she actually saw were very different. Yes, there were metal shelves full of toilet rolls, linen towels and bottles of disinfectant, but they seemed to be blurred. Perce couldn't make out their exact shapes. She blinked, trying to focus on the shelves, and moved forwards.

Suddenly, the cellar seemed to explode in a blast of heat. This was what she had felt when Mr Grimes had had his accident. From the far side of the store she could hear noises. Deep echoing moans were intermingled with high-pitched yells and screams. Perce froze, her heart pounding.

What was it?

Shaking with fear, Perce moved in further. By now the shelves had disappeared and Perce could make out a faint flickering light in the distance. This was too much! She turned to go back and gasped in horror. Instead of seeing the store-room, she saw a long stone tunnel illuminated by flaming torches. She panicked – this wasn't possible! The torches lit up a series of murals on the walls. Bright-red pictures showed bulls with people leaping over them.

Perce turned again, but in every direction she could only see more tunnels leading into the distance. As she spun around she could hear a roaring. She was trapped in a maze. This was a labyrinth! She had been right about O'Taur, but how could that help her now?

Almost fainting with horror, Perce stumbled back a step and flung a hand out to support herself against a tunnel wall. Something sharp and cold dug into her palm.

The shock cleared Perce's head. She was clutching a metal shelf! Something seemed to be tugging her onwards, into the labyrinth. The bulls that adorned the walls seemed to be staring down and mocking her: "You can't escape, you can't escape!" She could only see the rough rock walls of the tunnel, but she could *feel* shelves. Whatever her eyes were showing her, her fingers were telling her she was still in the cellar.

Closing her eyes firmly, Perce twisted, turned, stumbled and groped her way along the shelves, tripping over mops and buckets until at last she found the smooth roundness of the doorknob beneath her fingers. Perce yanked the cellar door open, staggered up the steps, and with an over-whelming sense of relief gasped in the safe and welcoming cold air of the playground.

"Where've you been?"

"What's wrong with her?"

Perce looked up. Still dazed, she could make out the shapes of Eddie and Well'ard making their way home from the gym club.

"O'Taur . . . labyrinth . . . bulls . . . proof . . . in there," gibbered Perce, pointing at the cellar. Eddie stared at her in amazement.

"She's been at the wine-gums again," said Well'ard.

"No . . . in there, it's terrible. We've got to get help."

Before they had a chance to protest, Perce dragged them both towards the staffroom. She tried to tell them about O'Taur, and the labyrinth, but she kept getting mixed up and leaving things out. Eddie and Well'ard couldn't make head or tail of the rambling account Perce tried to give them, but her terror was unmistakably real. By the time they had reached the staffroom, Eddie and Well'ard had got hold of the idea that Lee and

Syreeta were trapped in the cellar, and in some sort of danger.

Eddie knocked on the grey staffroom door and they waited for someone to answer.

"There's got to be someone there!" moaned Perce.

"Even if there is, will they believe us?" asked Eddie. Well'ard stared at him and nodded.

"Leave it to me." He hammered on the door, with his fists, arms and finally his feet.

"What on Earth are you doing?" The door jerked open. Mr Latimer stood glaring.

"Sir, sir, it's an emergency!" yelled Well'ard, waving his arms about. "We've seen smoke coming from the caretaker's store. It could be on fire!" He turned and winked at Eddie. Perce was impressed with Well'ard's ability to invent stories in a microsecond. Years of practice she thought.

"Are you sure?" Mr Latimer eyed the three kids suspiciously. Well'ard was the school's All-Time-Lie-Telling Champion and Eddie had a bigger imagination than Steven Spielberg – but Perce? "All right," he said, "I'm coming."

They took the short cut through the kitchens,

clattered down the steps, and stood before the cellar door.

"There's no sign of smoke." Latimer peered at the door. There was a pause. He glared suspiciously at Perce.

"There's no time to explain, sir," cried Perce, "There's something terrible in there and I can prove it! Look!"

Perce turned the doorknob and flung the cellar door open.

"Good evening, Mr Latimer. What can I do for you?"

Perce stared in horror. There were no flickering torches, no heat, no noise, no labyrinth; just shelves, buckets, mops and, sitting calmly at his desk, reading a newspaper, Mr O'Taur.

Chapter Eight

ARE YOU READY, EDDIE?

As they picked up litter in the yard next day, Well'ard and Eddie complained bitterly that Perce had got them into another fine mess. Perce insisted that it wasn't HER fault.

"Oh yeah?" sneered Well'ard. "Who was it then who talked us into dragging Latimer down to the caretaker's store with some cock-and-bull story about a Greek monster in a lavvy-plinth . . ."

"Labyrinth," corrected Perce.

Well'ard scowled. "What is a laby-thingy anyway?"

"It's an underground maze," Perce explained. "It's where the Minotaur lived."

"Yeah?" Eddie was impressed. "What, like secret passages and stuff?"

"That's right. It was at Knossos . . ."

"Bless you."

"I wasn't sneezing, you wally!"

Perce explained that the Labyrinth of Greek mythology was in Crete. King Minos had ordered a giant underground maze to be built beneath his palace. People Minos didn't like got shoved down into this Labyrinth, and they got lost . . .

". . . and wandered around until they died of starvation and turned into skellingtons, right?" Well'ard watched too many Indiana Jones movies.

"Wrong. Until the Minotaur got them."

Eddie and Well'ard shivered.

Andy wandered past. He pretended he hadn't seen Perce.

"Anyway, I reckon that's what happened to Lee

and Syreeta and the others. They got into the Labyrinth."

Well'ard scratched his head. "But you said the Labyrinth was in Crossness."

Perce tried again. The Labyrinth was in *Knossos*. In Crete. Well'ard was still puzzled. Why, he wanted to know, was the Labyrinth in a crate? Perce head began to ache. No, it wasn't in a crate. Knossos was a place in *Crete*. Crete was an *island*. In the *Mediterranean*. The Mediterranean was a *sea*.

Well'ard still wasn't happy. "Yeah, well, what I meantersay is, how can it be there and here as well? Eh? Cleverclogs?"

Eddie interrupted to ask why, if Perce had got into the Labyrinth through the cellar, it hadn't been there when they took Latimer to see it.

Perce thought hard. Perhaps, she said, the Labyrinth wasn't there all the time.

This baffled Well'ard. He didn't understand how something could be there one minute and gone the next. To be honest, neither did Perce.

Eddie had another question. "If there is a Minotaur, what's it doing in our school cellar?"

Perce had an idea about that. "What if the

arrival of Ms Dusa opened some sort of door, so that other things could come through? I mean, other monsters from the Greek myths? What if O'Taur found that door?"

"So what does he want with Lee and Syreeta?"

Perce's patience ran out. "How am I supposed to know? Perhaps I can find something out in the town library. I'm going there after school."

"If we ever get this litter picked up," moaned Eddie.

"Litter!" complained Perce bitterly. "What a waste of time! If we left it, it'd still all be gone by morning. O'Taur would see to that."

"I reckon," said Eddie thoughtfully, "Latimer feels guilty about leaving stuff for O'Taur to clear up, so he gets us to do it."

"But it's O'Taur's *job* to clear up!" complained Eddie. "That doesn't make sense."

"It's how teachers think," pointed out Eddie, "it's not *supposed* to make sense."

This was an unanswerable argument, so nobody answered it. Anyway, just then the bell went for the end of break.

During the dinner hour, while Perce and Andy were working very hard at ignoring each other from opposite ends of the school-yard, Well'ard took Eddie to one side.

"Lissen," he said round a mouthful of bubble gum, "what d'you reckon to this Minotaur lark? You reckon Perce could be right?"

Eddie looked blank. "Well, what if she is?"

"What if we found the Labyrinth an' this bull-bloke? We'd be heroes, wouldn't we?"

"Yeah," breathed Eddie. His technicolour imagination was immediately flooded with front page stories in the paper, TV interviews and victory parades . . .

"What about it, then?"

"I'm in." Eddie's face fell. "Hey, but it's no good."

"What isn't?"

"Well, they won't believe us, will they? All the teachers have got this weird idea that I exaggerate things. And they think you tell lies."

"Me?" asked Well'ard, the picture of injured innocence. "Why?"

"Because you do tell lies," said Eddie bluntly. "All the time."

"Only to teachers," protested Well'ard. "That's not tellin' lies, that's misleadin' the enemy."

"It's teachers we've got to convince."

"Huh!" said Well'ard, nettled. "Teachers! Fancy not believin' you, just 'cos you tell lies."

For a while, Eddie thought and Well'ard sulked.

Eventually, Eddie's face lit up. What he and Well'ard needed was a witness to go and find the labyrinth with them: someone who the teachers would listen to: someone who didn't tell lies.

"Flamin' 'eck," grimaced Well'ard. The thought of someone so depraved they never told lies made him feel quite peculiar. "Where can we find someone like that?"

Eddie suggested Jane Flamstead.

"Biggest liar in the school," said Well'ard glumly. "She told me she saw Elvis Presley fryin' cod at the Ocean Wave Chipperama."

"She never!" Eddie was shocked. "If you can't trust a kid whose dad's a vicar, who can you trust?" He brooded for as moment and then said, "She didn't see him, really, I s'pose?"

"Nah." Well'ard was scornful. "I went and looked. Nothin' like him."

Eddie sighed. Then he brightened. "Hey, what about Claire Greene? She comes to the gym club with her mate."

"Huh! Grassy Greene! She's shopped so many people she ought to be called Sainsbury's."

Eddie agreed, but the point was that the teachers believed everything Claire said. That was exactly the sort of witness they needed. All Well'ard had to do was to get her down to the cellar . . .

"How'm I supposed to do that?" Well'ard protested. "She wouldn't go anywhere with me. She'd think I was goin' to thump her." He considered. "She'd be right an' all."

Eddie looked cunning. "Tell her you saw some older kids smokin' in there."

"D'you think she'd come then?"

"Is the Pope a Catholic?"

Well'ard's brow furrowed. "I dunno. Is he?"

Eddie rolled his eyes. "Just tell her. Straight after school, OK? I'll see you by the cellar steps."

At home-time, Perce made a bee-line for the town library, and was soon poring over a book on Greek Mythology.

In some accounts of the legend, read Perce, the Minotaur is said to be King Minos's son Asterius, or Asterion. Others say the Minotaur was Minos himself. All the legends agree that the monster lived in the Labyrinth under Minos's palace.

The people of Athens had lost a war against Minos, so he made them pay him a tribute. Every nine years, seven young men and seven young women were sent to be sacrificed to the Minotaur.

Prince Theseus of Athens offered to be one of the sacrifices . . . .

Perce read on and made notes until she reached a passage in the book that made her snap the point off her pencil. Shocked, she carefully re-read the section:

One of the most interesting things about the whole Minotaur legend is the bull dance . . .

As Perce read on, her eyes grew round with horror.

Eddie's plan worked. Nearly.

Well'ard told Claire he'd seen a few older kids sneaking into the cellar with a packet of ciggies, and an avenging gleam appeared in her eye. But she refused to investigate without her friend Stacey.

Well'ard reckoned that was OK. Two witnesses were better than one — that's what Well'ard's brother said and he should know. He was in court often enough.

The first thing they saw when they rounded the corner of the yard was Eddie, dressed in knee britches, white stockings, a velvet jacket, a little black hat with Mickey Mouse ears and a red cloak draped over his shoulder.

Well'ard's mouth dropped open. "What are you got up as?"

"The local Operatic Society left it here when they performed *Carmen*. Good, isn't it? I'm a matador."

Well'ard glowered. "You look more like a doormat."

Eddie struck a pose. "Zey call me, El Macho."

"You're sure it's not El Plonko?"

Stacey giggled while Claire eyed Eddie with dis-

83

trust. "What's he wearing that for?"

"Beautiful *senorita*, I dedicate ze ears of zis bull to you."

Well'ard dragged Eddie to one side. "What are you playin' at?"

"We're going to fight a bull, aren't we? So I'm going to be a bullfighter."

"Well'ard!" Claire hissed. "What about these boys you saw going . . ."

"Yeah! Right!" Well'ard gave Eddie a poisonous glance, and turned back to the girls. "Yeah, they're in there. I saw 'em. Def'nit'ly." He pointed down the steps to the cellar door.

Stacey shivered. "We ought to go and get a teacher."

"Ah, but then they might sneak out before you got back," said Eddie hurriedly, "but if you go in now you can see who they are."

Giving Claire no time to think about the holes in that argument, Eddie and Well'ard propelled the girls through the door.

Right until that moment, if they'd been honest, Eddie and Well'ard would have had to admit they'd been expecting to find themselves in the caretaker's store after all. Eddie even had a couple of stories in reserve, one for the girls, and one for Mr O'Taur if he happened to be in there.

Once they were through the door, though, they found themselves in a tunnel of rock. There wasn't a mop or a toilet roll in sight.

Eddie and Well'ard were almost as startled as Stacey and Claire.

"This isn't right." Claire's eyes grew round. "I'm sure it shouldn't be like this . . ." She broke off as the door slammed shut behind them with a crash that echoed down the tunnel. They were plunged into darkness. Stacey grabbed Claire's arm. Well'ard only just stopped himself from grabbing Eddie's.

"It's the wind," quavered Well'ard. "It must've got up and blown the door closed."

"The door isn't the only thing that's got the wind up," muttered Eddie.

As the echoes faded, a red glow appeared in the distance.

"There you are, see?" Well'ard pointed. "It's all right. That's probably the boilers."

Nobody looked convinced, but there was no

going back, so they went on. After only a few steps, they came to a point where the tunnel split. The red glow seemed to come from both directions.

"Which way now?" asked Claire.

As if in answer, the red glow suddenly burst out of the tunnels like flame. Blasts of hot air blew at them, sending them clawing blindly out of the way. Eddie and Well'ard staggered out of the blast, took to their heels and ran, stumbling, coughing, desperate to get away from whatever was down in the Labyrinth. Eddie tripped over something, and fell, shrieking . . .

. . . and landed on something soft.

The something soft was Well'ard.

Eddie blinked and looked about. They were both sprawled in the middle of a scattered pile of toilet rolls. Somewhere in the corner a mop fell over with a clatter.

They were back in the caretaker's store.

The door stood slightly open.

Eddie looked around. "Claire?" he called softly.

Well'ard sat up, dislodging toilet rolls. "Where are they?"

"I dunno." Eddie called again, louder this time. "Claire? Stacey?"

But there was no reply. Eddie and Well'ard had staggered out of the Labyrinth alone.

Of the girls, there was no sign.

Chapter Nine

WHAT A DRAG!

"All right, where is she?"

Andy folded his arms and glared at Eddie and Well'ard.

"Who?"

"Perce! She put you up to this, right? 'Go and tell Andy some old rubbish an' we'll have a good giggle', right?" He peered over their shoulders, looking for Perce's hiding-place. "She's going to jump out and yell 'Gotcha!', right?"

Eddie gave Well'ard a helpless look. They had rushed from the cellar straight to Andy's house and poured out the whole story.

"It's true!" yelled Well'ard. After a lifetime of telling lies, and usually being believed, he was now telling the truth and being accused of lying! How unfair could life get? "We did see it, the tunnels an' the torches an' the pictures an' everything!"

Andy stared hard at him. Written on Well'ard's face was something that Andy had never seen there before: honesty. Usually when Well'ard told a lie he looked too innocent. What's more, he really was scared stiff; and Well'ard wasn't scared of *anything*.

Andy humphed. "Why come to me about it?"

"We thought that you could . . . er . . . tell us what to do," explained Eddie.

"You should ask Perce," said Andy bitterly. "She's the expert on mythical monsters." He tried to shut his front door. Well'ard got his foot in the way and grabbed Andy's shirt front.

"Lissen," snarled Well'ard. "It's true, the laby-thingy is there. We were there, in it, an' the girls *did* disappear. An' what about Syreeta an' Lee an' the others? How d'you think they feel about bein' chased through tunnels by a dirty great mad bull?"

"I should think it'd put them right off roast beef," said Andy.

Well'ard seethed. "Okay, wise guy. Let's go and see Perce."

"What if I don't want to come and see Perce?" inquired Andy loftily.

"Are you really that fond of hospital food?"

Andy blinked. "I'll get my coat."

Andy sat gazing out of the window. They were in Perce's lounge. Eddie and Well'ard were running through their story again, making slightly more sense this time. Andy still didn't believe it.

"We were well scared," finished Eddie.

"*You* were scared," snapped Well'ard. "I wasn't,"

"You said you nearly filled your pants and you weren't talking about putting on weight."

Well'ard gave Eddie a 40,000 volt look.

Perce's eyes were alight with excitement and she

was nearly bursting with the effort of not yelling "Told you so!" at Andy. "Never mind about who was scared! I think I've found out what O'Taur's up to."

She told them what she'd read in the library. Even Andy began to take an interest as Perce related the story of Theseus entering the Labyrinth with the help of Minos's daughter, Ariadne. All three boys particularly enjoyed the outcome of the story: the single combat between Theseus and the monster in the echoing depths of the Labyrinth, and the hero's defeat of the Minotaur.

"Anything else?" asked Eddie when Perce had finished.

"Nothing important," Perce lied. She thought it best not to tell them about the bull dance. There was no point in scaring them into fits.

Andy was still not convinced. "If it's true, then why aren't you all in the labyrinth now?" he demanded. "You've all been down there, so why didn't it capture you?"

Eddie was stumped and Well'ard didn't understand the question, let alone know the answer. It was left to Perce.

"I think it's all to do with the tribute – seven boys and seven girls." Andy looked puzzled. Perce carried on. "There are already seven boys in the labyrinth; Lee and the six who helped O'Taur put away the vaulting-horse. So it doesn't need any more boys – that's why Eddie and Well'ard got out. But there's not enough girls. Only Syreeta, and now Claire and Stacey."

"So why didn't you get taken, if girls are needed?" asked Andy, still trying to pick holes in Perce's theory.

"I think it *was* trying to pull me in: but I didn't actually go inside the labyrinth, I was sort of on the doorstep, still in the storeroom."

Andy kept quiet. It seemed to make sense and he couldn't think of anything else. It was left to Eddie to ask the question they had all been avoiding.

"So if the Labyrinth will only let girls in, how do we get in there?"

A slow, evil smile crept across Perce's face. Andy watched it in alarm. "Oh, no! Perce!" He tried to hide behind the sofa. "Don't even think about it . . ."

Perce's eyes glinted. "To make the legend work, the Minotaur needs four more girls. Me and you three . . ."

A look of horror spread over Well'ard's face."No way," he growled.

"We'd look stupid," protested Eddie, who was still wearing his matador costume.

Perce stared at him and raised her eyebrows. "Do you know how stupid you look *now?*"

"Anyway," protested Andy, "even if this Labyrinth does exist, and we do get in, what happens then?"

"We defeat O'Taur and rescue everyone," said Perce matter-of-factly.

"Oh, that's all right then," sneered Andy. "Such a brilliant plan is bound to work."

"I ain't going anywhere dressed as a girl," announced Well'ard.

By now Perce was desperate. She knew if she could convince Well'ard, the others would follow. "But Well'ard, they're not girl's clothes really," she coaxed. "They're a disguise." She had an inspiration. "Like the SAS wear."

Eddie perked up. "Yeah, like in World War II.

Prisoners were always dressin' up as nuns to escape. Well known fact."

"Like the SAS," said Well'ard, eyes wide open.

"Like the SAS," nodded Perce.

"Right, we'll do it!"

"Well'ard!" howled Andy, "noooo . . .!"

Chapter Ten

ALL STRUNG UP

The sight of Eddie, Well'ard and Andy walking towards school, dressed in Perce's clothes, caused several people to stop and gawp. Cats fled as they approached; mothers snatched their toddlers off doorsteps. A passing bus driver nearly wrapped his Number 47 round a lamp-post.

Well'ard had chosen a slinky top, with a pair of leggings. Both were black ("So I can't be seen in the tunnel.") They went well with his black combat boots and a set of fluorescent-pink love beads Perce's grandmother had worn in the Sixties when she was a Flower Child.

Eddie tottered behind in an old flowery dress that Perce's auntie had bought her (and Perce had refused to be seen dead in), and a pair of Perce's old wedgies.

"How do girls walk in shoes like this?" he muttered, as he staggered sideways and twisted his ankle for the fifth time in as many minutes. He shifted his schoolbag on to the opposite shoulder. He'd insisted on bringing his matador costume along. "After all," he had said, "you never know."

Perce grinned as she eyed Andy. "You look ever so nice."

"Just don't make any comments, okay?" Andy was wearing a pair of leggings with black and white horizontal stripes and a matching baggy T-shirt.

"I look like a bar code," he moaned.

"You look very fetching," cooed Perce.

"I'm warning you . . ."

The school gates were locked so they had to climb over the wall, which provided some amusement for Perce, but not for Eddie in the dress.

"Why do you wear things like this? They're not practical!" he cried as he attempted to stop the dress blowing over his head. Perce turned away. Eddie's stick insect legs and Mickey Mouse boxers were not a pretty sight.

Well'ard kept watch while the other three sprinted across the yard and down the steps to the cellar door. He needn't have bothered, the school was deserted.

"Right, here goes," whispered Perce as Well'ard joined them.

Steeling herself, she flung the door open.

They all stood and gaped. Beyond the buckets and mops, ghostly stone tunnels led off into the distance. Murals danced in the flickering torch-light. Deep in the tunnels pulsed a strange red glow.

"Sorry, Perce," said Andy in a small voice.

Perce nodded.

"Right, let's do it!" Well'ard pushed his way past the others towards the Labyrinth. As he stepped forward, the stone tunnels became less fuzzy and more solid.

"It's working. It's letting us in," Eddie cried out excitedly. He began to step forward.

"Wait!" ordered Andy. "How do we find our way out again?" Three pairs of eyes turned expectantly towards Perce. She had the answer.

"The same way Ariadne helped Theseus escape. She gave him a ball of string. He tied it at the entrance of the Labyrinth and unwound it as he went along, so when he wanted to get out, all he had to do was follow the string."

"And have you brought any string?" asked Eddie.

Perce shook her head. "Andy has, though. He's always got string in . . . his . . ." She tailed off.

"Great!" Andy threw his hands in the air. "Yeah, I always keep string in my pockets, only my pockets are in my jacket over at your house, and here I am, thanks to your big idea, looking like a . . ."

"There must be some in here," interrupted Perce. "There's bound to be some string in a caretaker's store."

But there wasn't. Luckily, Eddie had a brain-wave. "What's soft, strong and incredibly long?" he asked.

"Your nose," suggested Perce.

"No – this." He held up a roll of toilet paper.

"Brilliant!" cried Perce. "Eddie, sometimes you're a genius."

Eddie beamed.

"But usually you're a div," said Andy.

As the four of them made their way through the tunnels of the Labyrinth, Eddie unwound the toilet roll behind them. He'd tied the end to the cellar doorknob.

The painted bulls followed their progress through the stone tunnels.

Andy looked at the bulls. He shivered as a sound that might have been a distant roar echoed through the tunnels. He wiped sweat from his forehead. The roar and the heat – all as they'd said. Next time he'd believe Perce – maybe. "Still," he told himself, "it might not be anything to do with O'Taur."

"What's that!" Well'ard's shout caused everyone

to stop.

"I don't know."

"I heard something."

"So did I," yelled Eddie.

"RUN!"

The four of them shot off down the tunnel, Eddie leading the way, left, right, forward, twisting and turning through the ways of the Labyrinth.

"STOP!"

The four of them ground to a halt.

"Why are we running?" asked Perce, gasping for breath.

"Well'ard said we should," replied a wheezing Eddie.

"I didn't!"

"Did!"

"Stop bickering!" ordered Perce. "It's nothing. We just panicked. All we've got to do is go back to where we were. Follow the loo paper."

"Ah," said Eddie. There was a pause. "You know this paper is supposed to be soft, strong and incredibly long?"

"Yeah?"

"Well, two out of three ain't bad. It's soft and incredibly long, but . . ."

He raised his arm to show the others.

The toilet roll had snapped.

Chapter Eleven

THE BULL DANCE

They trudged on through the maze of tunnels.

There was nothing else to do. They had long ago lost all trace of the way out. At first, they had hunted high and low for the loose end of toilet roll, but finally had to admit that for all they knew, they could have been moving further away from it rather than towards it the whole time.

The tunnels seemed to go on for miles, with the flickering torches set along them at intervals. On every wall, painted bulls charged; but as they looked more closely, Andy, Well'ard and Eddie could see that there were pictures of people on the wall, too. They were slim and strong, dressed in short kilts and tunics. They ran around the bulls, and seemed to be flying over them.

Well'ard nudged Perce. "'Ere. What they doin'?"

Perce was looking straight ahead down the tunnel. "Who?"

"Them. In the pictures."

"Er . . . dunno . . ."

Perce's tone of voice made Andy's ears prick up.

"What is it you don't want us to know about?" he asked.

"You don't want to know about it."

"Come on, Perce." Andy planted his feet and folded his arms. "Give."

Perce stopped dead, and sighed. "OK, OK." She sat down with her back against one wall of the tunnel. Andy sat opposite her. Eddie sat on his school-bag. Well'ard stood.

"The people in Crete called it the bull dance. It's what happened to the seven boys and seven girls that Athens sent to the Minotaur as tribute."

"They made them dance round the bull?"

"Not exactly *round*. More sort of . . . *over*. More sort of . . . *on*."

Well'ard sat down too; his legs had started to feel all wobbly.

"Are you saying they used to dance with the bulls?" Andy was aghast.

"Look at the walls."

The pictures suddenly looked menacing. Once they'd heard Perce's story, it was clear what was going on. The human figures were boys and girls, jumping over the bulls.

"You know that stuff O'Taur had us doing, with the vaulting-horse? And the handlebars?"

"Look, they're . . . they're vaulting." Eddie's shaking finger traced the patterns of the leaping figures. "They're doing vaults over a socking great bull . . . and they're using the horns as *handgrips!*"

Andy shook his head in sheer disbelief. "Perce, it's not possible. Nobody could jump over a charging bull, it can't be done."

"OH, BUT IT CAN!"

The huge, deep voice echoed up the tunnel. Perce, Eddie, Well'ard and Andy gave each other one horrified look, and screamed.

The tunnel *tilted* beneath them. Scrabbling with hands and feet, they were tipped inexorably down as the slope increased. Gusts of hot air buffeted them, their ears were full of roaring, and they tumbled headlong into the red glow that rose from the depths to engulf them.

They landed in a crumpled heap. After a few seconds' groaning, they looked cautiously about.

They were lying in a great cavern. The air seemed to burn and throb. To their right, stood a massive stone slab. A huge bull's head was carved into the rock wall above it.

To their left, a great stone throne rose out of the rock. In it sat a terrifying figure; powerful muscles glistened in the fierce red glow. The creature on the throne, though human from the neck down, had the shaggy head and curving horns of a monstrous bull.

"**Welcome**," rumbled the Minotaur.

Perce felt her stomach churn with terror. If you looked closely, she thought, you could see that the Minotaur was Mr O'Taur, in the same way that you could see a family likeness between a Dachshund and a Dobermann; it was just that the Dobermann was a lot bigger and fiercer and very much more likely, if you tried to pat it, to have your arm off. She gave Andy a sidelong glance.

"There's your pal O'Taur," she whispered. "Still think he's the greatest?"

Andy looked sick. "Isn't it funny how you can go off people?" Then he pointed. "Perce, look!"

On the other side of the cavern, standing as if in a trance, were Lee, Syreeta and the others; Claire, Stacey and the boys from the gym club. They were all dressed in loose kilts and tunics like the figures on the tunnel walls.

Instantly, Perce's anger returned. She swung to face the monster on its great carved throne. "What are you going to do to them?" she demanded.
"**You would do better to ask**," the Minotaur boomed, "**what I am going to do to you**."

He – or *it* thought Perce – stepped down from the throne and walked towards them. The floor shook. Eddie and Wellard made a spirited attempt to back right through the solid rock. The Minotaur towered over the struggling figures.

"**You will join me in the bull dance, you and your friends.**" The creature gestured towards its captives. "**You have been prepared for this.**"

Perce shook her head. "No."

The monster threw back its horned head and laughed until stones fell from the cavern roof. "**Do you believe you have any choice?**"

"But Theseus killed you!" Andy's yell of defiance brought the great head swinging round to him.

"**Theseus banished me.**" The roaring voice was dulled. "**He blocked the doorway from your world to my Labyrinth. But the wall between the worlds is thin, here. Another of my kind showed me a way through.**"

"Ms Dusa," whispered Perce. So she had been right about a doorway between the worlds. Hooray.

The monster nodded. "**We are the children of the gods, we creatures of myth. Do you think you can defeat one of us and not be called to account? After all,**" the cruel lips curled into a smile, "**we monsters must stick together.**" The monster raised its arms. "**You will all dance.**

Seven and seven will dance to the glory of the Minotaur."

"Ah, yes, but . . ." gabbled Eddie, ignoring the filthy looks he was getting from Perce and Andy, "there's supposed to be seven boys, yeah, and seven girls, right . . ."

"Only we're boys really," added Well'ard, "so it wouldn't be proper, us dancin' on bulls, 'cos we're not girls, we're . . . boys . . ." He tailed off.

The Minotaur moved in front of Well'ard. It thrust its great horned head down until its terrible breath made Well'ard's eyes water.

"**Tell you what,**" it said, "**let's pretend.**"

Chapter Twelve

A RED RAG TO A BULL

Perce stood facing the monster with Andy, Well'ard, Eddie and the other blank-faced captives behind her. Trying to keep her voice steady, she asked, "What happens now?"

"**We dance.**" The Minotaur nodded its great head. "**You must be swift and sure, for if you falter, you will be trampled to death.**"

"And if we get through the dance without falling?"

"Then you will be sacrificed on my altar to the greater glory of the Minotaur."

"That's not fair!" protested Andy. "If we can't escape either way, why should we dance to suit you?"

"Because you will not throw your life away. You will cling to it as long as you can, though you know what the end must be."

Before their eyes, the Minotaur began to change. Its back humped. It fell onto all fours. The glossy hair of its head spread along its arms and down its back.

Where the Minotaur had been, there now stood a gigantic bull.

Andy gulped. "That's a good trick if you can do it."

Perce watched the monster closely. "It's part man, part bull. We've seen it turned into a man, we should've known it could turn into a bull as well."

The bull pawed the ground. Its defiant roar shook the cavern.

Andy looked at Perce and sighed. "You dancin'?"

"You askin'?"

"I'm askin'."

"I'm dancin'."

The bull roared again, and charged. Perce raced to meet it.

Instinct took over. The session with the vaulting horse paid off. Perce leapt for the lowered horns, backflipped, sprang lightly off the bull's broad back, somersaulted and landed running. The bull turned.

The others were now coming into the fray. Andy faced the next charge, and a leap and a handspring took him over the bull's back. Well'ard followed. Eddie's clumsy spring left him sprawling, but the bull thundered on. Still in a trance, Lee, Syreeta and the others moved apart. The bull charged each in turn. They vaulted over it. The vaulting fell into a rhythm. Perce sprang, flipped, somersaulted again and again. The rhythm became a dance.

Gradually, Perce became aware that the bull moved slightly faster on every charge. At first, it had seemed easy – even exhilarating – to fly over the enormous, deadly creature in a perfect vault. But the vaulters were having to move faster every time, and make more complicated springs to avoid the bull's tireless rushes. The vaulters were not tireless. What had started almost as a game was now a test of endurance. The bull wasn't playing with them any more. Perce's arms ached, her feet were like lead. All around her, heads were drooping. The Bull Dance, complex and beautiful though it was, was a dance of death.

Perce saw Syreeta stumble, and twist aside in the nick of time. "Someone's not going to make it," she thought, "someone's going to be trampled to bits. And it's going to be soon." For a moment, she almost despaired. Then, from some hidden ember of defiance inside herself, a sudden flame blazed. She ran to the edge of the cavern, grabbed Eddie's discarded school bag, and fumbled it open.

Andy joined her, panting. "I don't think I can do this much longer."

Perce's eyes gleamed. "You won't have to."

Leaving Andy speechless, she stepped into the centre of the cavern, carrying a roll of cloth. At the same moment, Eddie made a mistake. Always the least capable of the vaulters, he had missed his spring, and landed sprawling, winded and helpless. The bull turned, lowered its horns, and hurled itself forward to trample and gore its first victim.

Perce stuck two fingers in her mouth and gave a piercing whistle. "Hey, *toro!*"

The bull skidded to a halt. It tilted its head as if questioning what it saw.

Perce flicked the cloth she was holding, and it unrolled. She stood facing the bull, waving the red cape from Eddie's matador outfit.

"*Toro! Olé!*"

The bull lowered its head and charged. Andy held his breath.

Perce whipped the cape aside. The bull thundered past. Its hooves scrabbled at the rock as it tried to turn. Perce sprinted across the cavern.

"Here, *toro!*"

Again, the bull charged. This time, it was ready for Perce's side-step, and almost caught her, but Perce was too quick. Again, she sprinted across the cavern, and had taken a new position before the bull turned.

The bull grunted. Now it was mad. Any trace of human intelligence had left it. It was an animal, and it wanted to kill. This time, it would not fail.

The bull charged. Andy watched with his heart in his mouth, as it bore down on the tiny, defence-less figure.

At the last possible moment, Perce flicked the cape away. Andy gave a sudden yell of triumph! Perce's last move had taken her to a position just in front of the altar. Distracted by the cape, the charging bull had failed to see its peril until it was much, much too late.

Still running at full pelt, the bull charged headfirst into the great stone altar. There was a sickening, crunching and splintering thud as horn, hide and bone met hard rock.

Andy punched the air. "Bull's-eye!"

Eddie whooped in triumph. "One hundred and eighteeeee!"

After that, things got a bit confused.

The floor trembled and great cracks ran across it. Stone slabs tilted beneath their feet. The walls quivered, and rocks fell from the cavern roof high above. The red glow of the Labyrinth blazed in fury; the heat was suddenly unbearable.

"It's an earthquake," yelled Andy.

"It's a cavequake," corrected Eddie.

Perce skipped sideways to avoid a falling rock. "Whatever it is, we want to be somewhere else."

Claire and the others were looking round in a daze, as if they'd just woken up from a nightmare and found that reality was much, much worse. Perce grabbed Claire and Stacey by the arms. "Get moving!"

Andy grabbed Lee, "Where?"

"Out!"

"Sounds good." Dragging Lee, Andy led a stumbling charge towards the nearest tunnel mouth.

The torches guttered and flickered as they staggered past. The roar of the collapsing Labyrinth, its dust and heat, pursued them as they fled up the tunnel.

"'Ere, did you do all that?" Well'ard asked Perce. His brain clearly hadn't quite caught up with events.

"I suppose so."

"Nice one!"

"The Minotaur said the Labyrinth was his

world," panted Perce, "so without him, it's falling apart."

"Is he dead then?" asked Andy.

"I didn't stop to take his pulse! Shut up and run."

"We're going the wrong way," howled Eddie.

"Keep going!"

"We'll never get out," sobbed Stacey.

Perce and Andy did their best to keep the line moving, but everyone was bewildered and exhausted. People were dropping to their knees, slumping to the floor, giving up. Perce stared at them helplessly, and then a flutter of movement caught her eye. There was something white, waving in the blasts of hot air from the tunnel depths. She gave a cry of delight, and pounced on it.

Eddie stared. "What've you got there?" He looked more closely, and his eyes widened with delight. He elbowed Perce out of the way, and grabbed the end of a roll of toilet paper. "Oh, you beauty," he cooed, fondling it.

Claire gazed at him in horror. "He's stroking a loo roll!" she wailed.

"It's all right, Claire," said Perce sarcastically, "it's not against school rules."

"But why is he doing it?"

"Because it's showing us the way out! Come on!"

The schoolyard was crowded when they staggered out through the sagging cellar door and up the steps. There were all the kids who lived close to the school, who'd seen the clouds of dust belching out of the cellar and heard the roar of the collapsing Labyrinth. There were their mums and dads, one of whom had called the fire brigade. Fire officers were arguing about whether they were dealing with fire, flood or subsidence. The police were tying striped tape between things and shouting, "Move along there!"

A battered Renault squealed to a halt as Perce and the rest stood blinking in the evening light. Mr Latimer got out in his gardening trousers and bedroom slippers.

He surveyed the bedraggled group, taking in the shattered cellar door, Andy, Eddie and Well'ard's strange appearance, and the duststained Greek kilts and tunics of the others. His eyebrows climbed up his forehead.

"It had better be good," he said.

Perce sighed and sat down in a heap. "Over to you, Well'ard."

Well'ard turned to Mr Latimer. A look of absolutely transparent honesty spread over his face.

"Well, sir," he began to lie, "it happened like this . . .".

About the authors

STEVE BARLOW was born in Crewe but now lives in Somerset with his wife and cats. After working as a puppeteer, refuse collector and laundry van driver, he became a teacher of the performing arts, before turning to full time writing.

STEVE SKIDMORE was born in Leicester. He trained as a teacher and met Steve Barlow at a school in Nottingham nearly twenty years ago. They began writing plays for their students and haven't looked back.

"THE 2 STEVES" are Britain's most popular writing double act for young people, specializing in comedy and adventure. They perform regularly in schools and libraries, delighting audiences of all ages.

To find out more about "THE 2 STEVES" visit their website *www.the2steves.net*

Some other Barn Owl Books you might like to read

STONE ME!
by Steve Barlow & Steve Skidmore
Illustrated by Tony Ross
ISBN 1-903015-43-X £4.99

When a rather dramatic new supply teacher comes to the school called Ms Dusa and she wears a large turban over her hair, Perce and Andy get suspicious. After several children get turned to stone the duo realize they are right, this is indeed Medusa come into the 21st Century. As none of the grown ups seem to rumble as to what is happening, Perce and Andy decide that action needs to be taken and they are the ones to take it!

A hilarious take on the ancient Greek myth that is both entertaining and informative.

YOU'RE THINKING ABOUT DOUGHNUTS
by Michael Rosen
Illustrated by Sarah Tisdall

ISBN 1-903015 £4.99

It was cold, spooky and very boring. Frank hated Friday nights, sitting in the museum while his mum did the cleaning. He felt very alone . . . until the skeleton came over for a chat.

"How about a doughnut?" asked the skeleton.

"OK," said Frank.

And suddenly the museum didn't seem quite so boring any more.

But after a few chilling encounters with some of the skeleton's weird and wonderful friends, all Frank really wants is his mum.

YOU'RE THINKING ABOUT TOMATOES
by Michael Rosen
Cover by Quentin Blake
ISBN 1-903015-44-8 £4.99

A sequel to the very popular *You're thinking about doughnuts*.

Frank is back among the ruins of the past again, this time on a school trip to a stately home. When the black servant in an eighteenth-century picture starts talking to Frank, he isn't really surprised. The girl was Sheba but is sure that isn't her real name and calls herself "Not-Sheba". Frank agrees to help her find out who she is, helped on the way by a celebrity mad mummy, who is desperate to be a star, and various statues from India and some exploited Victorian workers.

Another witty, zany story that leads the reader through an unorthodox view of British hisory and the colonial past.